This Little Tiger book
belongs to:

_____

_____

_____

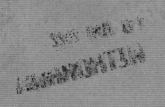

For Anna and Charlotte, with love ... xx ~ TC

For Matthew C, Dave T and Andy B, hands-on super dads!
And to all new parents – good luck ... ~ TW

LITTLE TIGER PRESS
1 The Coda Centre,
189 Munster Road, London SW6 6AW
www.littletiger.co.uk

First published in Great Britain 2013
This edition published 2013
Text copyright © Tracey Corderoy 2013
Illustrations copyright © Tim Warnes 2013
Tracey Corderoy and Tim Warnes have asserted their rights
to be identified as the author and illustrator of this work
under the Copyright, Designs and Patents Act, 1988
ISBN 978-1-84895-652-0
LTP/1400/0569/0313
Printed in China
2 4 6 8 10 9 7 5 3 1

NO!

Tracey Corderoy

Tim Warnes

LITTLE TIGER PRESS
London

Archie was adorable.
Everybody said so ...

Adorable
diddy-dum
dimples!

Then Archie learned
a brand new word...

Archie loved his brand new word.
So he said it more and more.

He said it at mealtimes...

He said it at bath times...

And he said it at every single bedtime...

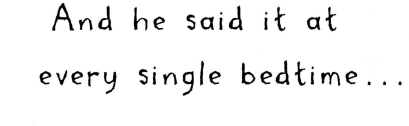

When it was time to go out Archie got himself ready.

But would he put his coat on?

Archie practised his new favourite word at nursery...

Can we play dinosaurs, Archie?

No!

Unfortunately, that
didn't go so well...

Soon Archie was saying his word **all** the time. But sometimes he wished he hadn't...

Come and join our train, Archie!

No!

Hey, where's everybody gone?

At home time, Daddy asked,
"Have you had a nice day?"
Archie gave a little sniff.

"Would you like a hug?" said Daddy.
"N-nnnnn..."

Now Archie had a
new favourite word ...

Hey, Archie!
Would you like
to play?

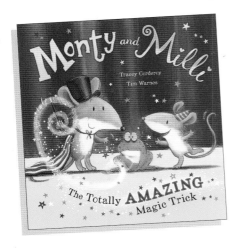

Monty and Milli
Tracey Corderoy
Tim Warnes
The Totally **AMAZING** Magic Trick

Bear's **Big** Bottom
STEVE SMALLMAN & EMMA YARLETT

Tracey Corderoy · Alison Edgson
Just One More!

Who's For **DINNER?**

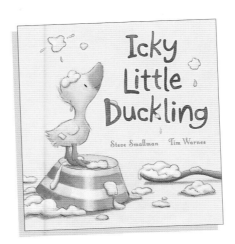

Icky Little Duckling
Steve Smallman · Tim Warnes

Paul Bright
Hannah George
If You Meet A **DINOSAUR**

More books you can't say **No!** to...

For information regarding any of the above titles or for our catalogue, please contact us:
Little Tiger Press, 1 The Coda Centre, 189 Munster Road, London SW6 6AW
Tel: 020 7385 6333 • Fax: 020 7385 7333 • E-mail: info@littletiger.co.uk • www.littletiger.co.uk